Here's what kids have to say about reading Magic Tree House® books and Magic Tree House® Merlin Missions:

Thank you for writing these great books! I have learned a great deal of information about history and the world around me.—Rosanna

Your series, the Magic Tree House, was really influential on my late childhood years. [Jack and Annie] taught me courage through their rigorous adventures and profound friendship, and how they stuck it out through thick and thin, from start to finish.—Joe

Your description is fantastic! The words pop out . . . oh, man . . . [the Magic Tree House series] is really exciting!—Christina

I like the Magic Tree House series. I stay up all night reading them. Even on school nights!—Peter

I think I've read about twenty-five of your Magic Tree House books! I'm reading every Magic Tree House book I can get my hands on!—Jack

Never stop writing, and if you can't think about anything to write about, don't worry, use some of my ideas!!—Kevin

Parents, teachers, and librarians love Magic Tree House® books, too!

[Magic Tree House] comes up quite a bit at parent/ teacher conferences.... The parents are amazed at how much more reading is being done at home because of your books. I am very pleased to know such fun and interesting reading exists for students.... Your books have also made students want to learn more about the places Jack and Annie visit. What wonderful starters for some research projects!—Kris L.

As a librarian, I have seen many happy young readers coming into the library to check out the next Magic Tree House book in the series. I have assisted young library patrons with finding nonfiction materials related to the Magic Tree House book they have read. . . . The message you are sending to children is invaluable: siblings can be friends; boys and girls can hang out together. . . .—Lynne H.

[My daughter] had a slow start reading, but somehow with your Magic Tree House series, she has been inspired and motivated to read. It is with such urgency that she tracks down your books. She often blurts out various facts and lines followed by "I read that in my Magic Tree House book."—Jenny E.

[My students] seize every opportunity they can to reread a Magic Tree House book or look at all the wonderful illustrations. Jack and Annie have opened a door to a world of literacy that I know will continue throughout the lives of my students.—Deborah H.

[My son] carries his Magic Tree House books everywhere he goes. He just can't put the book he is reading down until he finishes it. . . . He is doing better in school overall since he has made reading a daily thing. He even has a bet going with his aunt that if he continues doing well in school, she will continue to buy him the next book in the Magic Tree House series.—Rosalie R.

MAGIC TREE HOUSE® #31
A MERLIN MISSION

Summer of the Sea Serpent

by Mary Pope Osborne
illustrated by Sal Murdocca

SCHOLASTIC INC.
New York Toronto London Auckland
Sydney Mexico City New Delhi Hong Kong

ISBN 978-0-545-38266-3

Text copyright © 2004 by Mary Pope Osborne.
Cover art and interior illustrations copyright © 2004 by Sal Murdocca.
Magic Tree House is a registered trademark of Mary Pope Osborne; used under license. All rights reserved. Published by Scholastic Inc., 557 Broadway, New York, NY 10012, by arrangement with Random House Children's Books, a division of Random House, Inc. SCHOLASTIC and associated logos are trademarks and/or registered trademarks of Scholastic Inc.

12 11 10 9 8 7 6 5 4 3 2 1   11 12 13 14 15 16/0

Printed in the U.S.A.   40

First Scholastic printing, May 2011

To Susan Sultan and Kathy Reynolds,
my guides to the Selkie Cove

Dear Reader,

Summer of the Sea Serpent is the third in a special group of Magic Tree House books called "The Merlin Missions." In these books, it is Merlin the magician who sends Jack and Annie on their tree house adventures, often to mythical and legendary lands.

In the first Merlin Mission, Christmas in Camelot, Jack and Annie journeyed into a world of magic and fantasy to find a secret cauldron that held the Water of Memory and Imagination.

In the second Merlin Mission, <u>Haunted Castle on Hallows Eve</u>, they traveled to a mysterious castle. With their friend Teddy, they saved the future of Camelot by finding the stolen Diamond of Destiny.

Now, eight months later, on the first day of summer, Jack and Annie are about to go to a lonely seacoast in a fantasy land. They invite you to join them on their adventure. But beware—before night falls, incredibly strange things will happen. . . .

Mary Pope Osborne

CONTENTS

. . . King Arthur's sword, Excalibur,
Wrought by the lonely Maiden of the Lake.
Nine years she wrought it, sitting in the deeps
Upon the hidden bases of the hills.

Alfred Lord Tennyson
Idylls of the King

CHAPTER ONE

Summer Solstice

Jack was sitting on the porch reading the newspaper. It was a warm summer day, but the porch was shady and cool.

Annie poked her head out of the screen door. "Hey, Mom says she'll drive us to the lake this afternoon," she said.

Jack didn't raise his eyes from the weather page. "Did you know today is the summer solstice?" he said.

"What's that?" asked Annie.

"It's the official first day of summer," said

Jack. "There's more daylight today than on any other day of the year."

"Cool," said Annie.

"Starting tomorrow, the days will get shorter and shorter," said Jack.

A loud screech came from overhead.

"Look," said Annie, "a seagull!"

Jack looked up. A large white gull was circling in the bright noon sky. "What's he doing here?" asked Jack. "The ocean's two hours away."

The gull swooped down and screeched again.

"Maybe he's a messenger from Morgan or Merlin," said Annie. "Maybe one of them sent him to tell us the tree house is finally back."

Jack's heart began to pound. He put down the newspaper. "You think so?" he asked.

Jack and Annie hadn't seen the magic tree house since their Merlin Mission to a haunted castle last Halloween. Jack had begun to worry that the tree house might never come back.

"Look, he's flying toward the woods," said Annie.

Jack jumped up. "Okay," he said. "Let's go."

"We'll be back soon, Mom!" Annie called. Then she and Jack dashed across their yard. They ran down their street and into the Frog Creek woods.

The shady woods were dappled with sunlight. The air smelled fresh and clean. Jack and Annie hurried past the leafy trees, until they came to the tallest oak. High in the oak branches, the magic tree house was waiting for them.

"Wow," Jack and Annie said together. The tree house looked exactly the same as when they'd last seen it.

Annie grabbed the rope ladder and started up. Jack followed. When they climbed inside the tree house, no one was there.

"Look, our Royal Invitation is still here," said Annie. She picked up the card that had taken them to Camelot on Christmas Eve.

"And our leaf from Merlin is still here," said Jack. He picked up the yellow autumn leaf that had sent them on their Halloween mission.

"This is new," said Annie. She picked up a pale blue seashell. The shell was shaped like a small fan. There was writing on it.

"Hey, this looks like Merlin's handwriting!" said Annie. "We must be going on another mission for Merlin!" She read aloud the message from the magician:

To Jack and Annie of Frog Creek:
On this summer solstice, journey to
a land lost in mist, to a time even
before Camelot. Follow my rhyme
to complete your mission.

—M.

Annie looked up. "What rhyme?" she said.

"Let me see." Jack took the shell from her and turned it over. On the other side was a poem. Jack read the poem aloud:

Before night falls on this long summer day,
A shining sword must find its way
Into your hands and out of the gloom—
Or Camelot's king shall meet his doom.
To begin your quest for this Sword of Light,
Call for the help of the Water Knight.
Then pass through the Cave of the Spider Queen—

"Spider Queen?" Annie interrupted. She frowned. Spiders were about the only thing she was afraid of.

"Don't think about it now," said Jack. "Let's keep going." He read on:

. . . pass through the Cave of the Spider Queen
And swim with a selkie clothed in green.
Enter the Cove of the Stormy Coast,
Dive 'neath the Cloak of the Old Gray Ghost—

Jack stopped reading. "Old Gray Ghost?" he said.

"Don't think about it now," said Annie. "Keep going."

Jack read more:

Answer a question with love, not fear.

With rhyme and sword, your home is near.

Both Jack and Annie were silent for a moment. "That's a lot to do before nightfall," Jack finally said.

"Yeah," said Annie, "and I'm a little worried about the spider part."

"And the ghost part," said Jack.

"Hey," said Annie, "if we're going on another Merlin Mission, I'll bet Teddy will come with us! He can help us get through the scary parts."

"Right," said Jack. Just hearing Teddy's name made him feel braver.

"So," said Annie. "Onward?" *Onward* was Teddy's favorite word.

"Onward!" said Jack. He pointed to the handwriting on the pale blue shell. "I wish we could go to the time before Camelot!"

The wind started to blow.

The tree house started to spin.

It spun faster and faster.

Then everything was still.

Absolutely still.

CHAPTER TWO

The Water Knight

A salty breeze blew into the tree house. Seagulls screeched overhead. Jack and Annie looked out the tree house window.

They were high in the branches of a gnarled old tree. The tree was on a sea cliff beneath snowcapped mountains. The mountains overlooked a rocky coast. There was no sign of human life anywhere.

"It looks wild and lonely here," said Annie.

"*Really* lonely," said Jack. "I wonder where Merlin and Teddy are."

"I don't know," said Annie. "They were in the trunk of our tree last time. Let's look for them in this one." She climbed down the rope ladder.

Jack crammed the seashell in his pocket and followed her.

"Merlin?" Annie called. "Teddy?"

Jack and Annie circled the gnarled tree trunk, but there was no sign of an entrance into the magical chamber of Merlin the magician. They circled the tree again. Jack tapped the bark in several places.

"I have a feeling no one lives inside this tree," said Annie.

"I think you're right," said Jack.

"Maybe they're down by the water," said Annie.

Annie and Jack walked a few feet to the edge of the sea cliff and looked down at the rugged coast. They saw three coves, separated from each other by rocky cliffs. The cliffs were filled with shadowy crags and the dark mouths of caves.

In the first cove, sunlit water flowed from the open sea through a small space between the cliffs, then washed onto a pebbly shore.

The second cove was smaller, but looked much like the first.

The third cove was different. The farthest away, it was surrounded by a ring of bright green hills. A thin white mist hung over its milky-green waters.

"I don't see any sign of Merlin or Teddy," said Jack. "I guess we'll have to get started without them."

"Read the beginning of Merlin's rhyme again," said Annie.

Jack took the shell from his pocket and read aloud:

Before night falls on this long summer day,
A shining sword must find its way
Into your hands and out of the gloom—
Or Camelot's king shall meet his doom.

Jack looked up at the sky. The sun was almost directly overhead. "It must be around noon now," he said.

"We don't have much time," said Annie. "What do we do first?"

Jack looked back at the rhyme and read aloud:

To begin your quest for this Sword of Light,
Call for the help of the Water Knight.

"Oh, easy," said Annie.

"It is?" said Jack.

"Sure," said Annie. "If he's a Water Knight, he's probably down by the water." She started down the steep, rocky hill that led to the nearest cove.

Jack stuffed the shell back in his pocket. "But who *is* the Water Knight?" he yelled as he followed Annie.

"It doesn't matter," she yelled back. "We just have to go down to the water and call for his help."

They climbed over large boulders toward the cove. The boulders were slippery, but Jack's sneakers kept him from sliding. A damp breeze blew from the sea. It made his skin and clothes feel clammy.

When they got to the shore, Jack wiped the mist off his glasses and looked around. The wide beach was covered with silvery pebbles, shells, and rows of sea foam. Sandpipers and gulls picked at tangled ribbons of soggy seaweed.

"The tide must be out," said Jack. He studied the cliffs above the cove. "I don't know how a knight can get down here. A horse could never make it over all those rocks."

"Let's just do what the rhyme tells us," said Annie, "and see what happens."

Annie stretched out her arms. She closed her eyes. She raised her head toward the sky and shouted: "O Water Knight, whoever you are, come here and help Jack and Annie!"

"Oh, brother," Jack muttered to himself.

Suddenly they heard the wild cries of seagulls. "Jack, look!" said Annie. She pointed toward the middle of the cove.

Seabirds were screeching and flapping above a giant swirl of spray and foam. The swirl was spinning just above the surface of the water, headed toward the beach!

"Wow!" said Annie. She took off running across the sand.

"Come back!" shouted Jack.

"No! Come *look*!" said Annie.

Jack hurried to the edge of the surf.

Through the blur of spinning spray and foam, he saw the silver helmet of a knight appear above the water. He saw silver breast armor. Then a strange creature burst through the surface, carrying the knight on its back.

The creature had a horse's head and neck and front legs. But instead of back legs, it had a long, silvery fish's tail! With the Water Knight on its back, the horse creature half galloped and half swam through the cove. Seagulls shrieked wildly overhead, following the pair toward the shore.

As the knight drew close to the edge of the water, he looked straight at Jack and Annie. He raised his gloved hand and beckoned to them.

"Okay, we're coming!" cried Annie. She started pulling off her sneakers.

"Wait—let's think about this!" cried Jack.

"We don't have time!" said Annie. "He wants to help us. He's like the stag that came for us in Camelot."

"No, he isn't," said Jack. "He's much weirder!"

But Annie tossed her sneakers onto the

rocks and splashed through the shallow water. The knight held out his hand and helped her onto the strange horse creature. The creature slapped its fish's tail against the water, sending up a fountain of spray.

"Come on, Jack!" Annie yelled. "We can't waste time!"

Annie's right, Jack thought. They had to find the Sword of Light before nightfall. He pulled off his sneakers and tossed them up onto the rocks near Annie's. Then he stepped into the cold water and waded out to the knight.

Annie helped pull Jack up onto the horse creature. He sat on its scaly tail and clung to Annie while she held on tightly to the Water Knight's tunic.

The silvery fish's tail slapped the water. A shower of spray rained down on Jack. He closed his eyes. "Onward," he said faintly.

The Water Knight turned away from the shore. With more slaps of its tail, the horse creature began galloping and swimming across the cove. The seagulls shrieked wildly as they swooped after them.

Bumping up and down, Jack clung desperately to Annie. He kept his eyes squeezed shut and tried hard not to fall off.

As they sped across the cove, the Water

Knight guided his steed steadily over each ripple and wave. The bumpy ride soon turned into a smooth one.

"This is great!" cried Annie.

Jack opened his eyes. With the wind and spray whipping his face and hair, he began to feel more excited than scared.

"I'll bet he's taking us to the Sword of Light!" cried Annie. "We'll be done with our mission in no time!"

That would be too easy, thought Jack. But as they sped over the waves, he grew hopeful. *Maybe she's right. Maybe it will be easy*, he thought. *Not all our missions have to be hard. But what about the rest of the stuff in the rhyme? What about—?*

Before Jack could finish his thought, the strange horse creature stopped and reared up. Jack and Annie tumbled over its fish's tail and splashed into the cold water.

They sank for a moment and then bobbed

back up to the surface, frantically treading water. They looked up at the Water Knight and his horse.

The knight lifted his arm into the air. He pointed to a pile of boulders near the base of a nearby cliff. Then he spread the fingers of his gloved hand in a gesture of farewell.

"Bye! Thanks!" shouted Annie.

The horse creature slapped its fish's tail and took off in a fountain of spray and foam. With the gulls circling above them, the mysterious pair whirled toward the passage between the cliffs that led out to the sea. In a moment, they vanished into the open water beyond.

CHAPTER THREE

Cave of the Spider Queen

Gentle waves rippled through the cove as Jack and Annie swam to the foot of the cliff. They pulled themselves onto the boulders. Soaking wet, they sat for a moment in the warm sunlight and caught their breath.

"That was so cool!" said Annie.

"Yeah. But why—" Jack gasped, "why did he dump us way out here? What do we do now?"

"Check the rhyme," said Annie. "What happens after we call for the help of the Water Knight?"

Jack reached into his pocket and pulled out the seashell. He read aloud:

Call for the help of the Water Knight.

Then pass through the Cave of the Spider Queen.

"Oh. Right," said Annie. She took a deep breath. "Spider Queen."

"Sorry," Jack said softly. "But don't worry, maybe the Spider Queen is just a person. Maybe 'Spider Queen' is her nickname."

"But what if she's half a person and half a spider?" said Annie. "Like the Raven King was half a man and half a raven?"

Jack shuddered at the memory of the monster on their last Merlin Mission. "Don't think about that," he said. "Time's running out. Let's just find this cave."

Annie nodded and smiled bravely. "Okay, you're right," she said.

They stood up and started climbing barefoot around the craggy curves at the base of the cliff. As they rounded a corner, they both gasped.

In front of them was the mouth of a cave. The mouth was covered with thick, sticky white ropes. The ropes were woven tightly together in a crisscross cobweb pattern.

"If that's a spiderweb, we're in big trouble," said Annie.

Jack tried to sound calm. "Um, the size of the web doesn't actually tell us the size of the spider," he said. "Plus, I once read that no spider on earth is bigger than a dinner plate."

"Yeah, and no horse on earth has a giant fish's tail either," said Annie.

Good point, thought Jack. "Let's just concentrate on finding the Sword of Light before nightfall," he said.

Jack picked up a stone the size of a softball. He hurled it toward the mouth of the cave. The stone sailed through the giant cobweb and into the cave, pulling the sticky rope-like strands down with it.

Jack turned to Annie. "Ready?" he said.

She didn't move.

Jack took her hand. "Don't worry, I won't let any monster spiders get you," he said. He nodded toward the mouth of the cave. "Onward?"

"Onward," Annie repeated in a small voice. Then together she and Jack stepped over the fallen web and entered the Cave of the Spider Queen.

Inside the cave, the walls were black and shiny. The ground was wet and slippery under their bare feet.

"Yikes!" Annie said, jumping back. A pale pink crab scuttled sideways across the rocky floor.

"Don't be afraid," said Jack. "That's not a spider."

"I know," said Annie. "Sorry."

As they went deeper and deeper into the cave, it grew darker and darker. Finally Jack saw a faint light coming from a wide, arched passage. "That way," he said.

They stepped through the arch into a round chamber with a high ceiling. There were several large cracks in the ceiling that let in beams of sunlight. The misty light shined on mossy green ledges and on a green, spongy-looking floor. Silver droplets dripped from above, *ker-plopping* into tiny pools. Squeaks and chirps came from crannies and hiding places in the walls.

"What's that noise?" asked Annie.

"Probably just teeny cave crickets or baby bats," said Jack.

"No, *that* noise," said Annie, "the whispering noise."

Jack listened. Then he heard it: a low whispering. He couldn't make out the words. It just sounded like *whisper-whisper-whisper-whisper*. The hair stood up on the back of his neck. Now *he* began to feel scared.

"This place is really creepy," said Annie.

"No kidding," said Jack. "But we don't have to stay here long. The rhyme says we just have to *pass through* the cave. So let's hurry and pass through it."

Jack and Annie walked through the ghostly green light of the chamber. The spongy floor squished beneath their bare feet. As they searched for an exit from the cave, they both kept an eye out for the Spider Queen.

"Hey, look at the starfish," said Annie. She pointed to a bright orange starfish clinging to the rocky ceiling. "How'd *he* get up there?"

Before Jack could answer, a wave crashed into the chamber. Water splashed over Jack and Annie.

"Yikes!" said Annie. She and Jack jumped onto a mossy ledge jutting out from the wall.

The wave washed back out. There was a moment of quiet. Then another wave surged into the chamber. It splashed against the cave walls, soaking Jack and Annie again.

"Oh, man," said Jack. "The tide must be coming in! Soon this whole cave will be flooded!"

The wave receded. For a moment all was quiet again.

"We'd better leave *now*!" said Jack. "Quick! Go back the way we came in!"

Jack and Annie jumped down from the ledge. But before they could escape, another wave crashed into the cave! This one swept them off their feet and pulled them down into the foamy water.

Jack grabbed Annie's hand. Fighting the swirling current, they climbed back up onto the mossy ledge. The water churned and gurgled around the chamber.

"We can't go back the way we came in," said Jack. "The waves will just keep knocking us down, and we'll get caught in the current!"

"Maybe we can get out through that crack!" cried Annie. She pointed to the widest crack in the cave ceiling. It was high above the swirling water.

"It's too high!" said Jack. "We can't get up there!" He looked frantically around the flooded cave, searching for another way out. Suddenly he froze in horror.

Clinging to a ledge near the ceiling crack was the Spider Queen. She had eight red glowing eyes. She had eight long, hairy legs. And she was *much* bigger than a dinner plate.

The Spider Queen was bigger than Jack.

CHAPTER FOUR

Web Walk

Jack grabbed Annie's hand. "Whatever you do, don't look up," he said.

Annie looked up.

"AHHHHH!" she screamed. She started to leap off the ledge into the churning waters. But then another wave crashed wildly against the walls.

Jack held Annie back. "Don't jump!" he shouted. "You'll drown!"

Above the sound of the rushing waters, a loud whisper echoed around the cave: *Stay!*

Stay! Stay! The Spider Queen was staring down at them with her eight red eyes.

As Jack and Annie stared back in horror, the giant spider shot a web strand as thick as a rope straight toward them. Jack and Annie ducked. The strand stuck to the wall.

"What's she doing?" cried Annie.

"I don't know!" said Jack.

He and Annie looked back up at the Spider Queen. She'd crawled a few feet closer to the crack in the wall. She stared down at them for a moment with her glowing eyes, then shot out another thick rope strand.

"Watch out!" shouted Jack.

He and Annie ducked.

Thwack! The second web rope stuck to the ledge just a few feet away from the first.

"Oh, no! Look!" shrieked Annie. She pointed up at the cave ceiling.

The monster spider was zigzagging between

the two strands of her web. *She was heading straight toward them.*

Jack and Annie screamed and pressed themselves against the wall. "We have to leave!" cried Annie. But before they could make a move, another wave crashed into the cave! The water swirled with ferocious force around the chamber.

"We can't leave!" cried Jack.

"We can't stay!" cried Annie.

Wait! Wait! Wait! whispered the Spider Queen.

The giant spider kept zigzagging between the two lines, spinning more web, coming closer and closer and closer to Jack and Annie.

They watched in horror, unable to speak or move. But just when she came close enough to touch them, the Spider Queen turned and scurried back up to the ceiling, leaving a giant web ladder behind her.

The Spider Queen stared down at Jack and Annie with her eight red eyes. *Climb! Climb! Climb!* she whispered from her spot on the ceiling.

"I think she wants to help us!" said Jack.

"No! She wants to trap us!" said Annie.

The spider whispered again: *Climb! Climb! Climb!*

Something about her voice made Jack feel certain the Spider Queen wanted to help. "She doesn't want to hurt us!" he said. "She wants to help us escape! Besides, we don't have any choice!"

The water was rising higher and higher over their ledge. It was swirling above their ankles now.

"We have to climb her web!" said Jack. "I'll go first!"

He reached up and grabbed one of the spider ropes. It felt damp and sticky. He pulled himself onto the bottom strands of the web ladder.

"Grab on!" he shouted to Annie above the roar of the water. "We have to get to that crack in the ceiling!"

Annie grabbed one of the web ropes. "Eww!" she said. "It's gross!"

"Just climb!" said Jack.

Holding tightly to the sticky strands, Jack and Annie began making their way up the Spider Queen's web ladder. The web swayed and stretched, but it was sturdy enough to hold their weight. Its stickiness kept them from slipping and falling.

Crawling and climbing, they moved higher and higher above the crashing waters. As they drew near the crack in the ceiling, Jack kept his eyes on the Spider Queen. She was watching them carefully.

Finally Jack reached the ceiling crack. He swung to one side of the web ladder, putting himself between Annie and the giant spider.

"You go first," he said.

"Okay," said Annie. She grabbed the rocky edge of the opening and stuck her head out of the crack. "There's nowhere to go but into the water!" she called.

"How far down is it?" said Jack.

"Pretty far!" said Annie. "But I think we can make it!"

"Wait—" said Jack.

But Annie was already squeezing herself through the crack.

"Annie, be careful!" said Jack.

Splash!

"Oh, man," said Jack. He gripped the edge of

the crack. Then he glanced back at the Spider Queen.

Her glowing red eyes peered out at him from the shadows. *Go! Go! Go!* she whispered.

Jack smiled at her. "Thanks!" he said.

Go! the Spider Queen whispered again.

Jack pulled himself out of the darkness onto a narrow rocky ledge. The bright sun sparkled on the blue water of the small cove below.

"Come on!" Annie shouted. She was bobbing up and down on the gentle waves.

Jack took off his glasses. He pinched his nose and closed his eyes. Then he jumped off the ledge.

CHAPTER FIVE

Barrh! Barrh!

Jack splashed into the blue sunlit sea. He sank to the bottom and then bobbed back up. He coughed and pushed his hair out of his eyes.

Annie was treading water nearby. "Hey!" she called.

"Hey!" Jack sputtered.

"I was wrong! You were right!" Annie said. She sounded thrilled. "The Spider Queen just wanted to help us!"

"Yeah," said Jack. He shook the seawater off his glasses and put them back on.

"She must be really lonely!" said Annie. "She probably feels like she has to hide in that cave because she's so scary-looking!"

"Maybe," said Jack. He looked around the second cove. Purple shadows stretched over a rocky seashore beneath the cliffs. The sun had moved farther across the sky.

"We'd better hurry!" said Jack. "What do we do now?"

"Read the rhyme!" said Annie.

Jack pulled the shell out of his pocket. Treading water, he read the next line in Merlin's poem:

And swim with a selkie clothed in green.

"What's a selkie?" said Annie.

"Who knows?" said Jack.

He looked at the cliffs and the shore. *Is a selkie a fish? A person? What?* he wondered. Then Jack saw two dark shapes speeding like fat torpedoes below the surface of the water. They were coming straight toward him and Annie.

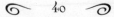

"Watch out!" Jack shouted.

"Yikes!" Annie yelled.

Jack and Annie swam out of the way as the creatures moved swiftly past them. Suddenly two sleek gray heads popped above the surface. They had wide snouts and long white whiskers. They had tiny, wrinkly ears and big, dark eyes.

"Seals!" cried Annie.

The two seals turned their heads like periscopes. When they saw Jack and Annie, they opened their mouths, showing their small, pointed teeth. They seemed to be smiling.

"Hi, guys!" said Annie.

Barrh! Barrh! the seals barked. Then they rolled through the water and bumped Jack and Annie with their noses. They barked again joyfully, then darted toward the shore.

"Come on!" cried Annie. "Let's play with them!"

"We don't have *time* to play!" said Jack.

But Annie had already started after the

seals, swimming toward the rocky beach.

"Annie! Stop!" called Jack. "We have to hurry and find the selkie! And the Sword of Light! Before nightfall! Or King Arthur will meet his doom. . . ." Jack's voice trailed off.

Annie didn't hear him. She and the two seals had reached the shore and were getting out of the water. The seals clumsily hauled their chubby bodies onto a big rock and flopped down. Annie climbed onto the rock, too.

"Annie, come on!" shouted Jack. *It could be as late as four o'clock now,* he thought. And there was still a *lot* they had to do before nightfall.

"Let's rest for a minute!" Annie called. She

sat near the seals and patted their shiny heads as if they were big dogs. The seals barked.

Actually, Jack wanted to rest, too. He felt really tired. *Maybe we could rest for a minute on the rock with the seals*, he thought, *then search for the selkie.*

"Well, okay," he shouted. "But just for a *quick* minute!"

Jack headed for shore. By the time he dragged himself out of the water, the seals were lying on their backs with their eyes closed. Their white whiskers twitched as they slept in the warm sunlight.

"Shhh, they're napping," said Annie. She lay down beside the seals and closed her eyes, too. "The sun feels really good, Jack. Come on. Lie down with us for a second."

"Oh, brother," Jack muttered. But the afternoon sunlight *did* feel good. He climbed onto the warm rock and lay down next to Annie and the seals.

"Okay, just for a *quick* second," he said.

Jack closed his eyes. The sunshine felt good on his tired arms and legs. The gentle sea breeze felt especially clean and fresh after the Cave of the Spider Queen. The next thing he knew, he had faded into a deep, peaceful sleep. . . .

CHAPTER SIX

The Selkie

"Wake up, lazybones! You can't sleep all afternoon!" said a friendly voice.

Jack's eyes shot open. *Oh, no!* he thought. *What time is it?* He sat up and looked around.

The seals were gone. Standing over Jack and Annie was a barefoot boy with a happy, freckled face.

"Teddy!" said Jack. For a moment he forgot all about the time.

"Teddy! Teddy!" cried Annie. She leaped up and hugged the young sorcerer.

Teddy grinned from ear to ear. He was wearing a brown tunic. His red hair was damp.

"You're finally here!" said Jack, laughing.

"I have been here for some time," said Teddy. "Merlin sent me early this morning. I was waiting for you on the beach when Kathleen came along and invited me to go for a swim with her."

Teddy turned to a girl standing a little farther down the beach. Like Teddy, she looked to be about thirteen. "Kathleen!" he called. "Come meet my friends!"

The girl smiled and began walking over the rocks toward Jack, Annie, and Teddy. She wore a green dress that looked as if it had been woven from grass. Her hair fell in black ringlets down to her waist like a dark waterfall.

"These are my good friends Jack and Annie," Teddy said to the girl. "They come from a far-away land."

"Hello, Jack and Annie!" the girl said in a bold, friendly voice. "I am very happy to meet you! My name is Kathleen." As she spoke, Kathleen's large eyes sparkled with the blue of the sky and water.

Jack couldn't speak. Kathleen was the most beautiful girl he'd ever seen.

"I like your dress," said Annie.

Kathleen laughed. "I wove it from sea grass," she said. "I am not a very good weaver, I am sad to say."

"Do you live here?" asked Annie.

"I do," said Kathleen, "with my nineteen sisters."

"*Nineteen* sisters!" said Annie.

"Yes," said Kathleen, tossing back her long curls. "I am the youngest of us all. We live in a cave up in the cliffs."

"Cool," said Annie. "Is your cave like the Cave of the Spider Queen?"

"No, no," said Kathleen. "It is much more cheerful than Morag's cave."

"So that's her name," said Annie. "I'm worried that she might be lonely."

"Ah, do not worry," said Kathleen. "Morag has many friends—bats, crabs, starfish. But it is kind of you to be concerned about her." She smiled at Annie.

Kathleen's friendly manner finally gave Jack the courage to speak. He cleared his throat. "The Water Knight was really cool, too," he said.

"The Water Knight?" said Kathleen.

"Yeah," he said, "the guy who carried us across the first cove."

Kathleen looked puzzled.

"His horse had a fish's tail!" said Annie.

"How strange," said Kathleen. "I often swim in that cove, but I've never seen or heard of such a knight."

"Have you lived here a long time?" asked Annie.

"Always," said Kathleen.

"Kathleen is a selkie," said Teddy.

"A *selkie*?" said Jack and Annie together.

"Yes," said Kathleen, laughing.

"You're in Merlin's rhyme!" said Annie. "It says, *Swim with a selkie clothed in green*."

"Merlin's rhyme?" asked Teddy.

"Merlin gave us a rhyme to help us find the Sword of Light," said Jack.

The smile left Kathleen's face. Her beautiful eyes darkened. "You have come in search of the Sword of Light?" she said. "Oh, dear. . . ."

"What's wrong?" said Jack.

"Many have passed through here seeking the Sword of Light," said Kathleen. "But as soon as anyone enters the cove beyond the Jellyfish Cave, terrible winter storms seem to burst out of nowhere. Even in summer, the storms have icy winds and rain. No seekers of the sword have ever survived these gales."

"Have *you* ever been to the cove beyond the Jellyfish Cave?" asked Jack.

Kathleen shook her head. "My older sisters have always forbidden me to go there," she said. "In fact, *no* selkie has ever dared swim into the Cove of the Stormy Coast."

"Cove of the Stormy Coast?" said Annie. "That's the next line in Merlin's rhyme! *Enter the Cove of the Stormy Coast!*"

"What *is* Merlin's rhyme?" asked Teddy.

"Here," said Jack. "Look."

He handed the seashell to Teddy.

The boy sorcerer quickly read Merlin's

message and rhyme. Then he looked at the sky.
"The sun moves on," he said. "Let us make
haste! We must find the sword before nightfall!
Or someday Arthur will meet his doom!"

"Wait a minute," said Annie. She looked at
Kathleen. "The rhyme says we're supposed to
swim with *you*. Will you come with us?"

Kathleen looked at them for a long moment.
Then she stood up and tossed back her curls.

Her eyes were bright. "I have always wanted to explore that cove," she said.

"Hurray!" said Teddy. "You will be the first selkie to do so! A grand adventure awaits us all! Onward!"

"Hold on," said Jack. "What about that Jellyfish Cave?"

"You need not worry about the jellyfish," said Kathleen. "They cannot harm us."

"They cannot?" said Jack.

"No," said the selkie, "not if we all change into seals."

CHAPTER SEVEN

Cove of the Stormy Coast

"Seals?" asked Annie.

Jack looked at Teddy. "Did she say 'change into seals'?" he asked.

"Indeed!" said Teddy. "That's what selkies do. They are people on land and seals in the sea."

"You're a seal?" Jack asked Kathleen.

"Sometimes," said the selkie, smiling.

Jack just stared at her. He couldn't believe the beautiful girl was sometimes a seal.

"Whenever I come ashore and dry off in the

sun, my seal skin falls away," said Kathleen. "Then I am as human as—well, as I am right now."

"Oh, I get it!" said Annie. "You were one of the seals we met in the water!"

"Of course," said Kathleen, "and Teddy was the other."

Jack looked at Teddy. "Y-you?" he stammered. "How . . . ?"

Teddy grinned. "I am a magician, remember?" he said.

Kathleen laughed. "Yes, but this time, 'twas *my* magic that did the work," she said. She pointed to two shiny gray skins lying on the sand. "I gave him a seal skin and spoke a selkie spell."

"You turned Teddy into a seal?" asked Jack.

"Aye," said Kathleen, "and I shall do the same for you. I am sure my sisters will not mind if we borrow two more of their skins." The selkie started toward a large pile of rocks.

Teddy watched Kathleen go, then looked back at Jack and Annie. "She has powerful magic indeed," he said.

"No kidding," said Annie.

Jack was speechless. He couldn't believe he and Annie were about to become seals.

Kathleen came out from behind the rocks carrying two shiny skins. "Take these," she said, handing them to Jack and Annie. The skins looked like scuba divers' wet suits with hoods.

"Pull them on over your clothes," said Kathleen. "Like this." She and Teddy picked up their own seal skins from the sand and began pulling them on. Jack and Annie did the same.

Jack stretched the skin up over his legs and shorts, then over his arms and T-shirt. He felt as if he were wearing a thick layer of rubber.

"Before we cover our heads and faces, we must wade into the water," said Kathleen. "Follow me."

Jack waded clumsily into the water with the

others. *This is crazy*, he thought. *You can't become a seal just by putting on a seal costume.*

Kathleen stopped them when they were waist deep. "Slip on your hoods," she said. "I will say a few words in selkie language. Then we shall all dive in."

Teddy grinned at Jack and Annie. "We have flown together through the sky," he said. "Now we shall swim together in the deep, eh?"

Jack nodded, but he still didn't believe this could possibly work.

"Quickly!" said Kathleen. "Cover your heads and faces! Dive as soon as I've spoken the spell!"

Jack pulled on his hood. He stretched it down over his forehead, then over his face—his glasses, nose, and chin. He couldn't see or talk. He wanted to rip the hood off, but Kathleen's voice stopped him:

An-ca-da-tro-a-day-mee!
Ba-mi-hu-no-nay-hah-nee!

Jack heard one splash—then two more. He quickly dove into the sea.

As soon as the seawater covered his head and body, Jack felt the seal skin melt into his

own. His chest expanded to the size of a barrel!
His arms and legs vanished and flippers took
their place!

Jack shot through the water like a torpedo.

When he moved his front flippers, he turned right or left. When he moved his back flippers, he zoomed forward.

Jack rolled and swerved in and out of schools of fish and jungles of sea grass. He dove down to the murky depths of the cove. Then he shot back up to the surface. In his smooth seal body, he could swim ten times faster than he ever had in his human body! And he could see and hear perfectly!

Jack rose and fell and rose and fell through the deep. Two seals appeared beside him. Bubbles came from their mouths. They made gurgling, clicking sounds. Jack could understand exactly what their seal sounds meant.

Hey, Jack! It's me!

'Tis me, too!

Hi, guys! Jack called to Annie and Teddy. He heard trilling sounds on his other side. He saw a third seal. It was Kathleen, swimming gracefully toward him.

Hello, Jack!

Hello, Kathleen! Jack clicked back to her.

He wanted to tell the selkie how much fun he was having. But when he opened his mouth, a school of tiny fish swam down his throat. Before he knew it, Jack had swallowed all the fish whole! But he didn't mind. He laughed a seal laugh full of bubbles.

Onward, Kathleen! clicked Teddy. *Lead us to the Jellyfish Cave!*

CHAPTER EIGHT

Cloak of the Old Gray Ghost

The four seals paddled with ease through the sunlit waters of the Selkie Cove and into the Jellyfish Cave. The water in the cave was cold and murky. But in his seal body, Jack was warm; and with his seal eyes, he could see clearly.

As they swam farther and farther into the cave, the jellyfish began to appear. At first there were just a few. Then there were hundreds . . . then thousands . . . pink jellyfish, purple jellyfish, orange and chocolate-colored jellyfish . . . jellyfish as big as umbrellas and

as small as pennies . . . jellyfish shaped like bells, saucers, parachutes, mushrooms, cannonballs . . . jellyfish as bright as candle flames and jellyfish as clear as glass.

Some of the jellyfish pulsed in and out as they swam. Others silently drifted by, their long stinging tentacles trailing behind them. As Jack swam among the jellyfish, he wasn't afraid at all. His tough seal skin protected him completely.

Finally Kathleen led Jack, Annie, and Teddy through a narrow passage of the cave and into the milky-green waters of the third cove.

The four seals poked their heads above the surface of the water and took deep gulps of air. Jack's whiskers twitched as he looked around the Cove of the Stormy Coast.

The cove was completely silent. It was lit with a hazy, warm light. The water was flat calm, without a single ripple. Circling the cove were strange green hills that shimmered in the afternoon light. Snowcapped mountains loomed above the hills. Jack could see the tree with the magic tree house on a distant sea cliff.

Climb onto those rocks and dry off! Kathleen barked.

They all swam to a small rocky island in the middle of the cove. Jack hoisted his blubbery, tear-shaped body out of the water. He flopped beside the others and puffed and groaned. The seal body that had felt so graceful underwater now felt heavy and awkward.

Jack's skin began to feel tighter and tighter in the sunlight. Almost before he knew it, the skin had slipped from his body like old wrapping paper. He was human again—lying on the rock in his shorts and T-shirt. He sat up and pushed his glasses into place.

"That was great!" said Annie.

Jack looked at her. The same magic had happened to Annie and the others. They were all human again.

"Yeah, it was," Jack said happily. He looked

around. "And I don't see any signs of a winter storm here."

"No, but still, I do not like the looks of this place," said Teddy. The boy sorcerer frowned as he peered around at the cove. "It gives me the quivers."

Jack glanced anxiously at Teddy. If Teddy was afraid, something *must* be wrong. Teddy never acted as if he were afraid of anything.

"Well, the day wears on," Teddy said, looking up at the sinking sun. "Let us hurry ashore to find the sword, so we can leave this cove as quickly as possible."

"I fear our search may be difficult," said Kathleen. "Look."

A dense gray fog was rolling down from the mountains. As they watched, the fog hid the sea cliff where their tree house had landed. Within moments, the fog had completely covered the green hills. Then it swept over the windless waters of the cove.

"Oh, dear," said Kathleen. "The Cloak of the Old Gray Ghost is upon us."

"The Cloak of the Old Gray Ghost?" asked Annie.

"Aye, that's what we selkies call a very thick fog," said Kathleen.

"And that's a line in Merlin's rhyme!" said Annie. *"Dive 'neath the Cloak of the Old Gray Ghost!"*

Jack breathed a sigh of relief. "Gray Ghost" wasn't a ghost at all! It was just another name for fog. "So I guess we just go ashore and look for the sword under the fog somewhere," he said.

"The rhyme says we *dive*," said Teddy. "So perhaps we do not go ashore at all."

"Oh, right," said Jack. "Does that mean we get to turn back into seals?" Shivering in the cold fog, he was eager to slip back into his warm, protective seal body.

"I fear we cannot *all* be seals," Kathleen

said, "for how could we grasp a heavy sword
with our flippers?"

"You and Teddy be the seals, then, and look
for the sword," said Annie. "Jack and I can swim
down and grab it after you show us where it is."

Jack was about to say he'd rather be a seal.
But before he could speak, Teddy piped up.
"Excellent plan!" he said.

"Indeed," said Kathleen. "Your friends are very brave." She turned and smiled warmly at Jack.

"Uh, sure, no problem," he said.

"Let us make haste," said Teddy. Hidden by the fog, he and Kathleen pulled their seal skins back on. A moment later, Jack heard Teddy call out, "Farewell, friends!" Then Kathleen spoke her selkie spell. Her words were followed by two splashes.

"What do we do now?" Jack asked.

"We wait for them to find the sword," said Annie.

"I hope they hurry," said Jack, shivering.

"Me too," said Annie.

They listened for the barking of the seals. They listened and listened. . . .

"I wonder what time it is," said Annie.

"Impossible to tell," said Jack.

"They'd better—"

"Shh!" said Jack.

He heard a faint seal bark, then another and another. But in the thick fog, he couldn't tell where the barks were coming from. "Where are they?" he said.

"I think they're over *there*!" said Annie.

Splash! Annie had jumped in. Jack couldn't see her in the fog.

"Annie, where are you?" he shouted.

"Here!" Annie yelled through the ghostly mist. "Come on!"

Jack put his glasses down on the rocks. Then he slowly lowered himself into the water. As he started after Annie, his human body felt thin and frail compared to his powerful seal body. He couldn't swim nearly as fast. He couldn't hold his breath underwater for nearly as long. And he was freezing cold.

The seal barks grew louder and louder. *Barrh! Barrh!*

Jack didn't see their two friends until he nearly bumped into them. Teddy and Kathleen were swimming in a tight circle, barking excitedly.

"Did you find the sword?" Annie shouted at them. "Is it here?"

The seals barked and dove under the water. Jack and Annie took deep breaths and followed.

The seals swam quickly to the sandy bottom of the cove. They circled a shimmering object sticking out of the sand.

It was the golden handle of a sword.

CHAPTER NINE

The Sword of Light

Annie pointed to the sword handle. Jack nodded. But he was running out of air. He swam back up to the surface. Annie followed him.

Their heads bobbed above the water, and they gasped. "Did you see it?" cried Annie. "The handle of the sword?"

"Yes! The blade must be buried in the sand!" said Jack.

"We have to pull it out!" said Annie. "And we have to hurry!"

"Right!" said Jack.

He and Annie took giant gulps of air. Then they swam back down to the bottom of the cove. Jack got to the sword first. He grabbed the handle and pulled. The sword didn't budge. He pulled again. The sword still didn't move.

Annie grabbed one side of the handle. She and Jack pulled together. Jack felt the sword move a tiny bit. His lungs felt like they were about to burst.

Gripping his side of the handle with both hands, Jack pulled with all his might. Suddenly the flashing blade slipped out of the sand!

Jack and Annie carried the sword up through the water as fast as they could. They burst into the air, clinging to the Sword of Light and gasping for air.

"We got it!" Jack called to Kathleen and Teddy.

The seals circled around them, splashing and barking joyfully.

Barrh! Barrh!

"Lead us to the rocks!" Annie shouted.

Jack and Annie each held on to the sword's handle with one hand. Paddling with their free hands, they dragged the sword after the seals.

As they swam, the fog began to lift, and the sky turned from gray to blue. By the time they reached the rocky island, light from the late-afternoon sun was again glinting off the strange green shoreline.

"Hold the sword while I get out!" Jack shouted to Annie.

Jack climbed onto the rocky island. He took the sword from Annie, then carefully pulled it up onto the rocks and laid it on its side.

Annie climbed out of the water. Nearby, Teddy and Kathleen poked up their seal heads. They were all silent as they stared in wonder at the sword.

"Wow," breathed Annie.

Jack nodded. The mighty sword reflected the burning light of the setting sun. Its blade glowed as if it, too, were on fire.

"Now what do we do?" Jack said.

"We have to get the sword to Merlin *fast*," said Annie. "The sun's about to go down."

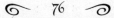

"Right," said Jack. "Before nightfall. Right."

Suddenly Teddy and Kathleen barked a warning. Jack and Annie looked up.

The water had begun to ripple. The ripples started at the edge of the cove and swelled toward the center. Waves crashed against the small rocky island, sending up great showers of spray.

"What's going on?" said Jack.

"Maybe a bad storm's coming!" said Annie.

Barrh! Barrh! Kathleen and Teddy tried to haul themselves onto the rock, but the waves pushed them away.

"We've got to help them!" said Annie. She and Jack tried to help the seals out of the rough water. Their hands slipped over the sleek seal skin, and they nearly toppled into the water themselves.

The waves kept rolling and splashing. *Barrh! Barrh!* The two seals were swept away from the rocky island.

"Look!" cried Annie. "The land is moving!"

Jack looked at the strange green shoreline surrounding the cove. It *was* moving! It shifted from side to side, then slithered forward!

A great roaring noise rocked the cove. A monstrous head rose above the surface of the water.

The green hills were not hills at all. *They were the coils of a giant sea serpent's body!*

CHAPTER TEN

The Ancient Question

"AHHH!" screamed Jack and Annie.

The giant sea serpent arched its long neck into the sky. Its scaly green skin glistened in the late sunlight. Staring at Jack and Annie, its eyes burned like bright yellow lamps.

Jack and Annie were frozen with terror.

The monster opened its mouth. Inside were hideous fangs and a purple forked tongue. The serpent made a terrible hissing sound!

Jack and Annie huddled together on the rock. Frantic seal barks came from far away.

"Teddy!" yelled Jack. "Kathleen!"

"Their magic can't help us now!" cried Annie. "They're stuck in their seal—"

Before she could finish, the sea serpent's deep voice boomed through the cove: "WHO ARE YOU? AND WHY ARE YOU SSSTEAL-ING THE SSSWORD OF LIGHT?"

Jack was too stunned to answer. But Annie shouted back at the monster. "We're Jack and Annie! We're on a mission for Merlin!"

"SSSSSSSSS!" the serpent hissed angrily. Its purple tongue flicked as it coiled its body around the rocky island. Then the monster arched its neck and lowered its huge head.

Again, the ancient voice boomed through the cove: "TO BE WORTHY OF THE SSSWORD, YOU MUSSST ANSSSWER THE QUESSS-TION OF THE SSSWORD."

"What is the question?" shouted Annie.

"SSSSSSSSS!" hissed the serpent. It turned away and circled the rocks again. Soon its scaly green body was coiled twice around the little rocky island.

It's going to crush us! Jack thought with horror. Maybe they had strength enough to stab the monster before it squashed them. "Pick up the sword!" he shouted at Annie.

Together Jack and Annie lifted the mighty sword. They gripped its handle and pointed the gleaming blade at the sea serpent.

"Don't come any closer!" Jack yelled.

The serpent came closer. Its eyes flashed. Its forked tongue darted in and out. It opened its mouth wide.

"Wait! Stop!" Annie shouted at the sea serpent. "Give us a chance! Ask us the question!"

The serpent closed its mouth. Then it arched its neck, and its huge head dipped down right in front of Jack and Annie. In a low, deep voice, it said, "WHAT ISSS THE PURPOSSSE OF THE SSSWORD? THAT ISSS THE ANCIENT QUESSSTION."

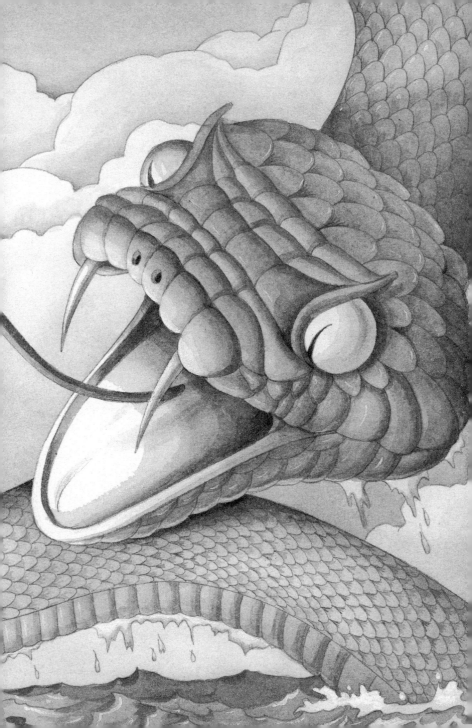

"Okay! The purpose of the sword! Just a minute!" shouted Annie. She turned to Jack. "What is the purpose of the sword?" she asked.

"To defeat your enemies?" Jack said.

Annie shook her head. "That doesn't sound right."

"To force them to give up?" Jack said. "To slay them?"

"No, I'm sure that's not right," said Annie.

"SSSSSSSS!" the serpent hissed at them impatiently.

"Then *what*?" said Jack.

"I don't know," said Annie, "but maybe— maybe it's not about fighting at all! Look at it!"

Jack stared at the gleaming sword. Its silver blade glowed against the red sunset sky. Staring at the wondrous sword, Jack felt calmer. A strange sense of joy and relief came over him.

"ANSSSWER THE QUESSSTION!" the serpent boomed.

Jack's mind became clear. "I think I've got it," he said. "Remember the line from Merlin's rhyme? *Answer a question with love, not fear.*"

"Yes!" said Annie. "That's it! It's not about fighting! It's about not being afraid!"

"ANSSSWER THE QUESSSTION!" the serpent boomed.

Jack looked up at the serpent's face. As he stared deep into its yellow eyes, he no longer felt any fear. It was the serpent who seemed afraid now.

"The sword should not be used to harm anyone or anything!" Jack shouted.

"That's right!" said Annie. "It should be used for good only!"

The serpent stopped swaying. It flicked its tongue.

"The sword should not make people afraid!" said Jack. "It should help take away their fear! If they're not afraid, they'll stop fighting!"

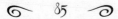

85

The serpent was very still.

"The purpose of the sword is not fighting!" Jack shouted. "The purpose of the sword is *peace!*"

CHAPTER ELEVEN

Sword and Rhyme

The sea serpent moved its head very close to Jack and Annie and hissed a long, whispery *ssssssss*.

The serpent's flicking tongue touched the sword for a moment. Jack's heart nearly stopped. But then the serpent slowly pulled back its head and began to uncoil itself from around the rocky island.

The monster kept uncoiling its great body, until once again one wide ring surrounded the cove like a circle of green hills. Then the serpent's head sank beneath the water with barely a ripple. It was impossible to tell where its body started and where it ended.

Jack and Annie lowered the Sword of Light and laid it back on the rock. Then they let out a huge sigh of relief and sat down next to the sword.

Kathleen and Teddy poked their seal heads up from the calm waters. *Barrh! Barrh!* they barked.

Jack and Annie laughed. "It's safe to come out now!" Annie called.

The seals hauled themselves onto the rocky island. Then they plopped on their sides.

"The sword helped us answer the ancient question," said Jack.

They all looked at the Sword of Light. It glowed brightly, even though the sun had slipped below the horizon and the purple sky was fading into twilight.

"We still have to get it out of here before it's completely dark," said Annie.

"I know," said Jack. "But how?"

"Look at Merlin's rhyme," said Annie.

Jack took the shell from his pocket. He read the last line of Merlin's rhyme:

With rhyme and sword, your home is near.

Jack looked up. "That doesn't make sense," he said.

"Perhaps it does," said Teddy.

Jack and Annie turned around. Teddy and Kathleen were standing behind them. Their seal skins had silently slipped off. They were human again.

"Perhaps it calls for a magical rhyme," said Teddy. "And I *am* a magician, remember?"

Annie laughed. "How could we forget?" she said.

Teddy grinned. "I have gotten much better at my rhymes," he said. "Just watch." He

rubbed his hands together. Then he carefully picked up the Sword of Light. He gripped its handle with both hands. He pointed the silver blade toward the tree house on the distant sea cliff.

Teddy took a deep breath. Then he shouted:

O Sword of Light, now light the night!

Teddy paused. Jack grew worried. Teddy always had trouble finishing his rhymes. And even the ones he did finish never worked the way they were supposed to.

Kathleen stepped close to the young sorcerer. "Say it again," she said softly.

Teddy called out again:

O Sword of Light, now light the night!

Kathleen finished the rhyme in selkie language:

Ma-ee-bree-stro-eh-brite!

The sword began to vibrate in Teddy's hands. There was a roar and a blast of white light. Shimmering beams shot through the dark. The beams wiggled and waved, then streamed together to make a glittering bridge.

The bridge spanned the purple darkness of dusk. It stretched from the rocky island in the middle of the cove to the sea cliff above the coast. When Teddy lowered the sword, the bridge remained in the sky.

"Wow!" whispered Annie. She turned to Kathleen. "What did you say to finish the rhyme?"

"*Ma-ee-bree-stro-eh-brite*," Kathleen told her. "*Make a bridge, strong and bright.*"

"Yes, that is exactly what I was going to say," said Teddy.

"Indeed," said Kathleen, smiling. She took Teddy's hand, then turned to Jack and Annie. "'Tis a bright bridge to take you from my world back to yours."

"You mean—we can walk on it?" said Annie.

"Try it," said Teddy.

"Oh, man," said Jack. He laughed nervously. Then he raised his foot and put it down on the

light. It felt solid. He put his other foot on the
light and took a step forward. The light felt as
firm as a brick pathway.

Annie stepped onto the light bridge beside
Jack. It was wide enough for them to stand side
by side. "This is so cool," she whispered.

"Wait, do not forget *this*," said Teddy. He carefully handed Jack and Annie the Sword of Light.

Together they gripped the handle of the sword. "What about you guys?" asked Jack.

"I must return to my cave now," said Kathleen, "or my sisters will begin to worry."

"And I will see Kathleen back home," said Teddy, "then return to the future in Camelot."

"After you stay for supper with me and my sisters," Kathleen reminded Teddy.

"Oh . . . ," said Jack. He wanted to have supper with the selkies, too. He wanted to spend more time with Kathleen and Teddy, whatever they were doing.

"We'd better get going, Jack," said Annie. "It's almost dark."

"Okay," said Jack.

"Good-bye for now," Kathleen said to them. "And thank you. 'Tis amazing how you defeated the enemy."

"The sea serpent wasn't really our enemy," said Jack.

"He was like the Spider Queen," said Annie. "They both seemed really scary until we got to know them."

"Yeah," said Jack.

"Will we see you again?" Annie asked Teddy and Kathleen.

"Yes, I have a feeling you will see both of us again soon," said the selkie.

"We will find you when you least expect it," said Teddy with a grin. "Now, my friends, you must go. Night comes quickly upon you. Farewell."

"Farewell," said Jack and Annie. They turned and started walking up the bright bridge. High above the water, the sword's light swung over the cove like a swaying lantern. The water below shimmered with sparkling ripples.

Jack heard two splashes behind them. He stopped and listened.

"Go, go, go," whispered Annie.

Jack started walking again. He and Annie climbed higher and higher, until they came to the end of the bright pathway.

They stepped off the bridge onto the rocky sea cliff above the coves. Clutching the handle of the sword, they looked back.

The shining bridge shattered into a million pieces of golden light. Like the sparks of a firecracker, the glittering pieces rained down through the sky. Then they quickly burned out.

The cove below was dark and silent—except for the distant barking of seals.

CHAPTER TWELVE

The Isle of Avalon

"**N**ow what?" Jack asked.

"Now I thank you," said a deep voice.

"Merlin!" cried Annie.

Merlin stepped out of the shadows. He wore his red magician's cloak. His long white beard shined in the radiant glow of the sword.

"You brought the Sword of Light out of the gloom just in time," he said, "before nightfall on the summer solstice."

"Why did we have to get it on the summer solstice?" said Jack.

"That is the day when the powers of the Ice Wizard of Winter are weakest," said Merlin.

"The Ice Wizard of Winter?" said Annie. "Does the sword belong to him? Did we just steal it from him?"

"No," said Merlin. "Long ago, the Ice Wizard stole the sword from the Lady of the Lake and brought it to his kingdom high above the North Sea." Merlin pointed to the snowcapped mountains beyond the rocky coast.

"The wizard soon discovered that the Sword of Light was useless to him, for the Lady of the Lake had placed a spell upon it that made it powerful only in the hands of worthy mortals. Still, the wizard refused to part with it. He buried it at the bottom of the cove."

"The Cove of the Stormy Coast," said Jack.

"Yes," said Merlin. "Only recently did the seabirds tell me of the sword's whereabouts. I knew I needed worthy mortals to retrieve it. So I sent for you on the summer solstice, when the

Ice Wizard could send no mighty storms to keep
you from finding it. He could only throw the
'Cloak of the Old Gray Ghost' over you."

"So the Ice Wizard sent the fog," said Annie.

"And did he put the sea monster in the cove,
too?" asked Jack.

Merlin smiled. "No. The serpent serves the
Lady of the Lake. Long ago, he secretly took it
upon himself to find the sword and guard it.
Should any mortals survive the wizard's storms
and gales, they still had to prove themselves
worthy by answering the serpent's question. I
believed you two would be able to answer the
question wisely. And I was right."

"Your rhyme helped," said Jack.

He and Annie carefully handed the Sword of
Light to Merlin.

"Will you put this sword in a stone now?"
asked Annie. "So Arthur can pull it out someday
and become king?"

"No, *this* sword is even more powerful than

the sword in the stone," said Merlin. "This sword has a name—Excalibur."

"Excalibur!" said Jack and Annie.

"I will take it back to the Isle of Avalon now," said Merlin, "and return it to the Lady of the Lake. Someday after Arthur is king, she will give it to him. The sword will help him face many challenges bravely and wisely. He will—"

Merlin was interrupted by a strange sound from the water below. It sounded like the deep bellow of a foghorn.

"What was that?" said Jack.

"Ah, yes, there is one last thing to do," said Merlin. He raised the sword and pointed it toward the Cove of the Stormy Coast. Like the beam of a giant searchlight, the sword's light streamed over the black waters.

Merlin moved the beam back and forth, as if he were looking for something. "Ah," he said. "There he is."

The light revealed the gigantic head of the sea serpent. Its yellow lamp-like eyes shined back at them.

"He mourns now," said Merlin, "for he has lost his purpose for being here. 'Tis time we help him home to the waters of Avalon."

The magician lifted the sword slightly. The beam made a path to show the monster the passage out of the cove. The giant serpent slid through the water and soon disappeared beneath the waves of the dark summer sea.

"His mission is done now," said Annie.

"Yes, and so is *yours*, my friends," said Merlin. "You must climb the ladder to your tree house and go home."

By the light of the sword, Jack and Annie found their way to the rope ladder and climbed up into the tree house. When they looked out the window, they saw Merlin standing in the glow of the Sword of Light.

"Bye!" Jack and Annie called.

The magician raised his arm and spread his fingers in a wave of farewell. Merlin's gesture stirred something in Jack's memory, but he wasn't sure what it was.

"Let's go now," Annie said.

Jack took the seashell out of his pocket. He pointed to the words *Frog Creek*. "I wish we could go home!" he said.

"Wait!" said Annie. "Our shoes! We left them on the beach!"

Too late.

The wind started to blow.

The tree house started to spin.

It spun faster and faster.

Then everything was still.

Absolutely still.

Jack opened his eyes. A warm summer breeze wafted into the tree house. The noon sun shined between the tree leaves. No time at all had passed in Frog Creek.

"Merlin was the Water Knight," Jack said.

"What?" said Annie.

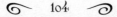

"When he said good-bye, Merlin gave us the same wave the Water Knight gave us," said Jack. "Remember?" Jack raised his hand and imitated Merlin's gesture.

"You're right!" Annie laughed. "Why didn't I think of that? He always helps us get started on our missions."

"And now we have three things from him," said Jack. He put the pale blue shell on the floor next to the Royal Invitation and the yellow autumn leaf. Then he looked at Annie.

"Home?" he said.

She nodded.

They climbed down the rope ladder and started walking barefoot through the damp, leafy woods.

"I guess we'll just have to tell Mom we lost our shoes in a time before Camelot," said Jack.

"Yeah," said Annie, "on our way to get the Sword of Light that was stolen by the Ice Wizard

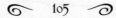

of Winter and guarded by a giant sea serpent who served the Lady of the Lake."

"Right," said Jack. "A simple explanation."

"You ready to go swimming at the lake now?" asked Annie.

Jack remembered the thrill of being a seal and zooming through the deep waters. "It won't be the same without Kathleen and Teddy," he said. "We won't be seals."

"We can pretend," said Annie. "Let's hurry before Mom decides it's too late to go."

They took off running. They ran barefoot through the woods, over sticks and leaves, through the dappled noon light. Then they ran down their street. They were out of breath by the time they reached their yard.

"Oh, wow!" said Annie. "Look!" She pointed at their porch.

Sitting in front of the door were their sneakers.

Jack and Annie climbed the porch and picked up their shoes. As Jack turned his over, fine white sand fell out—and a couple of tiny silver pebbles.

"Who—how?" he said.

A seagull screeched overhead. They looked up. The gull screeched again, then flew away and disappeared into the soft summer light.

Annie shrugged. "A little leftover magic," she said. Then she called through the screen door, "Mom! We're ready!"

A Note from the Author

Once again, details of old stories from Ireland, Wales, Scotland, and England have inspired a Magic Tree House Merlin Mission. While researching *Summer of the Sea Serpent*, I read about mythical creatures known as *selkies*, who were said to dwell in the inlets and bays of the British Isles. Selkies were "seal people" who took human shape whenever they slipped off their seal skins. In several old tales, female selkies marry fishermen and cause great heartache when they return to their seal lives.

Many Celtic tales also tell of water horses

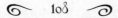

that live in Scottish lakes and of the legendary Gray Man, a bearded giant who spreads his fog cloak over lonely Scottish and Irish coasts.

Stories of giant sea serpents appear in tales from all over the world, from ancient Greece and Europe to India and Asia. Long ago, when the ocean was a realm of mysteries and marvels, many sailors and fishermen reported seeing long-necked, snaky monsters swimming in the deep. It's likely that they mistook giant squid, sea turtles, or whales for these sea monsters.

And of course, while working on this book, I was again inspired by the tales of King Arthur and Camelot, which have been told again and again over the centuries. For instance, my sword bridge was inspired by a sword bridge in the French tale "Lancelot," in which the knight has to cross a bridge created by a magic sword to reach the Isle of Glass.

In many versions of the tales of Camelot,

Arthur is given the mighty sword Excalibur by the Lady of the Lake, who lives on the Isle of Avalon. The sword's name may come from the Latin word *chalybs*, which means "steel." Some sources indicate that Excalibur was also known as the "Sword of Light."